MY HUMBLENESS LAID BEFORE ME

© Copyright 2025 Belinda Gaines

For more information, email
2424Belinda@gmail.com

Cover and interior design by
J. Daniel Gourdine

Published by

AngelGirlPublications.com

DEDICATION

To my family and three children, thank you for your full support and love.

My friends, thank you for supporting me on this journey to becoming an author.

DEAR READER

It is my heart's desire that through my efforts, you can escape and lose yourselves in my words.

It is my hope that you connect with those words and, when appropriate, cry, laugh, and even get angry!

At the end of every story, I hope that you say,

"That was powerful!"

"There is no greater agony than bearing an untold story inside you. Nothing will work unless you do."

--Maya Angelou

"You may not control all of the events that happened to you, but you can decide not to be reduced by them."

--Maya Angelou

My Humbleness Laid Before Me

My life. I was raised in the hood. Poverty.

I mean true poverty. Every building had three hundred units to its name. Each lot had three buildings. Over nine hundred families comprised men, women, and children. Also, poverty-stricken pets. The good thing about the poor cats was that they would eat and kill the mice. They were hungry, too. The dogs had no chance. They would sometimes eat food from the outside garbage bins and mice.

The building had roaches and mice running in and out. Mice droppings were everywhere—in the hallways and inside units. When you opened the elevator when it was working, three or four mice rode it to the lower level. It was bad.

Let's not talk about the black mold in units and on the walls of the buildings. My mama would clean the walls with bleach every three months, and then it would return. We would just have to deal with it. That's all we knew.

It was me, Tabby, Mama, and my little sister Tanya, whom we called Little T.

My mother was a short, 5-foot-5, heavy-set woman who wore her hair in two French braids. She also had those soulful, big arms that would wiggle when she waved goodbye. Let's not forget her signature nylons, which would always have the same run from the back of the knee down into her nurse-looking shoe. She always kept her uniform and nylons clean.

My mama was a single mother after my father got hooked on crack. While on crack, he started committing crimes, including burglary. He was finally caught. Now he is serving 15 years in prison. We didn't even go visit him. My Mama didn't want us to know what the inside of a jail looked like. She always said, "He made his choice." She made hers.

Mama worked two jobs, as a nanny and a maid.

That's all they had for a black woman who had little to no education. She had to drop out of school to manage her younger siblings and her alcoholic, party girl mother.

I heard all the wild stories about Nana. Every week, she would hang on the necks of different men, nasty men.

Also, in the clubs and bars every other night.

So, Mama had to protect her sibling from danger. She had to step into the role of mama.

Her childhood was cut short.

My mama had dreams. She wanted to be a nurse. She always wanted to work in hospitals, and she loved helping people.

She said she was called the "Hood Nurse" in her younger days. She always cleaned and bandaged the neighborhood children's scrapes and bruises.

Her dreams never came true.

Most parents around here today drink too much or party too much.

Women who worked did so as maids, cleaning other people's homes. They felt like failures. Yet, like my mama, they all wanted to provide more for their children. But in the hood, most couldn't.

Mothers and fathers drink liquor to drown their pain and sorrow. Mothers could be seen on the street, too intoxicated to realize their blouses were open, exposing their naked breasts. That was so common.

Our mama kept going; for us, she hoped things would be different one day for us.

Most black boys wouldn't go to school. Too busy shooting dice games on the corners and alleys.

Drunk old men on the corners would make sexual comments to me and my sister as we walked to and from school. I would say, "You old fart. Go inside and be with your wife and kids."

I had to be mean! That was the best way to keep them at bay, to protect my little sister.

I also cared for my sister and myself while Mama worked, trying to make ends meet. I was just a child, but I was responsible for keeping the home running. I was "Mama" in her absence. Very hard shoes to fill.

There was always some danger, one thing or another. Mice got through the cracks in the walls, loud music blasted daily, and young boys knocked on our door asking me to be their girlfriend. My response? "No! Get away from my door."

Kids ringing the doorbell and running away, called "doorbell ditch," which got on my nerves.

The apartment manager slid the rent late notice under the door more times than I could count.

Miss Williams and Miss Mildred always paid Mama late. That was stressful for Mama. They acted as though she were working for free, not caring about her responsibilities or obligations. Mom would leave every morning at 8:00 AM and return by 5:00 PM, right before the streetlights came on.

So, I would have all my homework done, and Little T would have hers done, too. Also, dinner would be done. I would always save Momma's plate. I knew she would be hungry. They sometimes worked her through her lunch period, thinking she did not deserve to eat or have a break. My Mama never complained. She was my hero.

A bath with Epsom salt was waiting for her to relax and soak away her aches and pains. She would be so grateful. She would kiss my forehead gently, saying, "What would I do without you, my rising star?"

She thanked me for everything I did, including household chores. My response was, "Mama, you take care of the family with everything you have."

She would always say, "Don't be like me. Be better. Make something of yourselves. Be Important one day."

Mama got that thought from a show on a black and white TV given to Mama by Miss Williams for Christmas. You could tell it was used.

It only had three stations: two, four, and seven. The rest was fuzzy, with lines running through it. Mamma often saw on Channel 2 where black women were nurses, librarians, teachers, dentists, etc. That fueled the idea that we could be somebody. You could because of education, education, and education.

Education was instilled in our brains as if it were major surgery. She would only get mad at us if our grades were lower than an A or B, or if we didn't finish our homework. We couldn't go to the playground on the weekends until we read a book and wrote half a page of what we read.

Even though Mama dropped out of school in the 10th grade, she knew when a paragraph sounded right and made sense. We could not fool her. We did it right, so we could all play at the park. She would always go with us because of all the evil characters who lived in the complex. She would die if anyone tried to hurt us.

At the park, that's the time momma could relax. She could breathe, look at her newspaper, and drink her coffee. Coffee is always made the same way: an ice cube, two tablespoons of brown sugar, one pinch of cream, and two pinches of cinnamon. Like clockwork.

We knew Mama was looking at the funny pages. We would glance and catch her smiling, but that was all right with us. Mama was just happy to be with us at the park, watching us slide, swing, and play in the sand. Her focus was only on us—no one else. That day, she was not a maid—just Mama.

We didn't love the ringworms we would get in our hair from the dirty sand. Mama threatened to ban us from the park quite often. She didn't have extra money to take us to the County Hospital. She would create old-school remedies for ringworms. She would mix Castor oil, hot sauce, and baking soda. Then, let it sit for 24 hours. It would burn and itch, but it would suck the life out of the ringworms. I guess they couldn't breathe or reproduce or spread. It worked every time.

She should have been a nurse. Many days, I would tell Mama, "Don't worry. I will get you out of the hood. I promise."

I fought just as hard as she did. It's all about getting our family out of the hood.

I worked and worked in school, becoming the "teacher's pet" in all my classes. I had to withstand racism. You could not be black and smart. Teachers would double-check my homework and classwork when I turned them in. They often asked, "Did you do this, or did someone else do it for you?" I would say respectfully, "I did it all." The teacher would say, "It's an A. But I'm watching you."

That made me feel terrible. They wanted me to fail. I witnessed the happiness and "great job" given to my few white classmates. One teacher said, "I did not know black people were smart." I would look at her with the side eye. Politely taking my "A's" straight home, waiting for Mama to come home and show her. "A's" always made her evening. She knew "A's" represented excellence. It made everything worth it.

Little T wasn't about education like Mama wanted. She got her homework done, but without the passion and hunger I had. She knew that without homework completion, she could not talk on the phone, watch TV, have her girlfriends over, etc., so she did what she needed to do to get by with B-minuses and C-pluses as the usual grades on her homework and tests.

Mama stopped fighting with her, but that was the lowest she could have. We continued to move forward. We survived the day-to-day happenings in the hood. We always kept our eyes open and our ears listening to the streets.

One day, Mama came home. She was so happy. She barely got through the door. She told us to come into the living room; she had something to tell us.

"Mama, what's wrong?"

"Nothing. God has answered our prayers. Miss Williams, my employer, sat me down and told me she needed more help from me to help with the kids since her husband was in that terrible car accident that left him temporarily unable to walk. It will take at least a year before he can start physical therapy. So, she asked us to move into her 2-bedroom and 1-bath backyard cottage. She said we could live there as long as we wanted and asked if I would be interested. I said yes! We would love to. We are finally escaping the everyday life of poor blacks. This black hole!"

"Mama for real?"

"We are out of here?"

"Yes, girls, we are out. We move in this weekend. I will be bringing boxes from the grocery store every day."

"Mama, I don't know what to say."

"Say nothing. Let's get out of here so you young ladies can become somebody. Remember, girls, let's run out of here."

The weekend came before we could blink. We were already packed when Saturday arrived. , the last box three floors down. The elevator was out of service more than it worked. Mama had walked up and down those stairs twice a day for years, even with groceries. Happy, Mama loaded and brought boxes down. She was a soldier. When she brought down the last box, she turned around and looked at the building one last time and began to cry.

"Why are you crying, Mama? Are you sad?"

"No, baby. I'm very happy because I knew we would get out of here one day, and today's that day. We can finally have the life we deserve. We will never return, and I have no regrets. You do what you have to until you can do better."

When we got to Westchester St., it was a whole other world. Clean streets, green lawns, nice cars, lovely homes, and areas for those of a particular color, and we know what that color is, white.

We were blown away when we opened the back gate to the cottage. It was beautiful and fully furnished, clean and bright. The living room had a color TV, the second bedroom had two twin beds, and the kitchen had a fully stocked refrigerator.

"This is our new home, girls."

"Wow, Mama."

"You guys go unpack and put your clothes up."

Mama went to the main house and knocked on the door.

"Miss Williams, we are here."

"Welcome. Come in. Are you OK with your accommodations?"

" Very much so. We are thankful and grateful. What is my new schedule?"

"OK, I need you to prepare the kids for school, cook breakfast, drop them off, pick them up from school, prepare dinner, serve it, and clean the kitchen. Then you are off. Your schedule Monday through Friday will be from 8:00 AM to 6:00 PM, OK?"

"I can do that. That is a fine schedule."

"Of course, you will still be off on the weekends. If an emergency occurs, I will need you to work, but I will pay you double your pay for that day. I don't anticipate that happening regularly. That's it for now. I have to go tend to my husband."

"Again, thank you, Miss Williams."

"You're welcome, Bessie, my dear. You are a loyal friend, and I will see you on Monday."

"Excuse me, Miss Williams. What school will the girls attend in this neighborhood?"

"Pardon me, your girls won't make it to our schools with what I assume are poor grades. So, they must catch the bus on the other side of town to continue at their current school. Malcolm X High School, I believe you mentioned to me before?"

"My girl Tabby gets all A's in school, and Tanya, Little T, gets B's and C pluses. The girls are doing pretty well in school. Education is the only way they can be somebody special."

"Well, I don't know about that. You should probably keep them there. That's what they're used to."

"I appreciate your suggestion."

As I walk away, I'm disheartened about her racist manner of speech. And I have to admit I am surprised. We had been friends since the kids were first born. Now, my girls are in the 8th and 10th grades. And it's great that their school starts in 8th grade and goes to the 12th grade. That way, they can go to the same school. They will stay there and finish out their school year. And they did just that. We stayed there for five years.

Life at the cottage was not always easy. Miss Williams' little girls, Samantha and Suzie, would talk to my girls and call them "black niggers" and tell them they were going to be their future maids when they grow up. Just like their mama.

The girls were gracious and mature. They would not even respond. Just give them the side eye. You know how black people do it. They knew they were going to flip the script. They would never use a mop and bucket if I had anything to say about it.

They worked hard. Tabby became valedictorian of her class, graduating with a 4.0 grade average. She did it, and her speech was beautiful.

"You of color can do anything. You just set your mind to it. You of color can overcome your upbringing and your environment's racism, even when it's thrown in your face up close and personal. You of color can rise above it all, even when people of a different color tell you that you will grow up and be their maid one day. I say I'm not going to be a maid. I'm going to be somebody. I will decide. I will decide. I am of color; I will decide who somebody I will be. You of color are me. Hold your head up high and rise. Rise, you of color."

She received a standing ovation from the audience and the school faculty. I, her mother, cried. I have never heard anything so beautiful. She enrolled at Los Angeles University.

I worked hard to graduate in three years, with my medicine degree and a business management minor. On graduation day, I dressed and put on my cap and gown. Mama took a picture of me and Little T, and then Little T took a picture of Mama and me. I had to leave to get my seat. I made it again as the valedictorian of my class.

I asked Momma and Little T to meet me at the graduation. The graduation was beautiful. This speech was short and sweet.

"I am, you are me, we are one. You can do whatever you set your mind to. Go do it."

"Mama, are you ok?"

"No. Not feeling too well."

As she was sitting, she fell to the ground. Little T screamed, "Call 911! Help!"

People in the audience moved chairs, fanned her, and provided CPR. An ambulance came and took her to the hospital.

Little T and I arrived at the hospital, ran to the nurse's station, and asked, "Where is my Mama? Miss Bessie? She was brought in by ambulance about 10 minutes ago."

"Let me check."

The doctor came out and walked towards us in slow motion.

"I'm sorry to inform you that your mother passed away. We could not save her."

I staggered, my mind reeling in disbelief. Little T fainted. I caught her as we both fell to the floor. Cradling her in my arms, I cried, sure that I would never stop.

The "Light" went out. Mama was our light. That was a brutal blow to me and Little T. Mama was gone in the blink of an eye. I was getting ready to be "Somebody."

I was advancing in my career. I was the chief of nurses and went on to become the director of nurses.

My Little T didn't do so well. Despite the love and support I gave her, I was not Mama. She felt she did not need to become somebody. She had no one to prove anything to. Her compass and navigator for life was gone.

She finished high school and one day said, "I'm leaving."

"Why? Don't go. Let me take care of you."

"I have my own people who have my back."

Of course, "her people" were those girls with gold teeth, long nails, long weaves, and bunny hop eyelashes. And the young street drug dealer.

You know the streets talk. My sister was in a relationship with Ducati, the number two street thug. He was her man.

When we did see each other secretly, she fit the description on the streets. We loved each other; we just operated in different worlds.

I know Mama would die if she saw the life she has now, but that was my little sister.

I was doing better than good. I had a beautiful home and a pool with a view of Beverly Hills. I went to the best restaurants. I had the finest clothes. I drove a black BMW M2 CS, a top-of-the-line sports vehicle, and I went up the ranks quite quickly. My degrees allowed me to be recognized. But it was not always easy to be accepted as a black, educated, intelligent woman.

I wore my hair in long, neat, sculptured braids. I have a slender build and a cocoa brown complexion. I loved me a double-breasted, wide-leg pantsuit, accompanied by my red-bottom, kitten-heeled pumps. That was me, all day long. Polished.

I outrank many of my white male and female co-workers. It wasn't easy for my counterparts to swallow that pill. I remember when I went to the hospital and attended my first meeting that I chaired. No one had known I was black, just Miss Tabby Thomas. As I walked in, no one, male or female, suspected I was the incoming chief of nurses. A young woman said, "Have a seat. We are all waiting for Miss Thomas."

I played the game and sat down for several minutes. People started to wonder why Miss Thomas was late, not knowing I was sitting among them.

Finally, I got up and said, "Hi, I'm Miss Tabby Thomas, Chief of Nurses."

They were shocked. All I saw were mouths to the ground, so to speak.

"Let's get started."

My agenda is on point. I informed the nursing department how it would run and the changes that would take effect in the next 30 days.

"I look forward to working closely with all of you. A team cannot thrive if we do not do our part. Thank you all."

That day was my first reality check about workplace racism. Everyone in the room was my white counterpart. I was disheartened that the only positions I had observed for people of color were housekeepers, dietary aides, and nurse aides. No person of color held a senior position.

Why would a home health aide be working at the hospital? I changed it to nurse aide.]

I was going to change that reality. I was also determined to rise through the ranks, whether they liked me or not. I had to be smarter, more educated, and hungrier. Always felt I had a target on my back. Eyes were watching every move.

I was offered the Director of Nurses position within one year of arriving. I was blown away. It came out of nowhere, which meant more money, a bigger office, a better parking space—a gigantic pay increase—and all the perks that came with the title.

Let's be clear. With more responsibility comes more stress. I now oversaw the entire nursing department; even seasoned doctors deferred to my expertise. Often, I would be the first one arriving and the last one leaving.

I had to make sure nothing slipped through the cracks. Remember the bullseye?

Ten years went by. I accomplished many achievements and received countless awards. I was proud of what I had done. I believe my Mama would have been proud of me. I was "somebody," as Moma would say. I made it.

As beautiful as it was, this wonderful lifestyle was very lonely at the top.

I don't have my sister right now. She's serving time in prison. She got caught up in the street life to the degree she was charged and arrested for having 5 kilos of cocaine with a street value of $127,500.

I hired her the best lawyer, but she still had to serve 5 years in the state pen—Lockhart Correctional Facility in Texas. And you know Texas isn't crazy about black folks. I did everything I could before she left. She told me she did not blame me.

"It's not your fault. My compass is broken. Please, remember that Big Sis."

I called her every Sunday and put money on her books. I sent her everything she needed. She was a rock star in there. I was so grateful that one of my nurses had a cousin who worked at the facility, and they were watching over her. She was very well protected. I was relieved. That was one less thing to worry about.

I have no friends, no male companion, just me and myself. Don't feel too sorry for me. This is the life I chose to live. In my determination to be somebody, I assumed I couldn't have it all: a family and a career.

Well, the pressure started to mount. More and more for me to handle. Putting out workplace fires weekly and, at times, daily. Pressure of not making any mistakes. The bar was set, and I set it. Coworkers around me were gunning for my job. Some try to sabotage me at work, undermine me, and challenge my decisions. I feel I'm always in defense mode. When I used to stay on the offense. Somehow, I'm losing. I always feel like I'm missing something. Something I haven't thought of. My mind won't let me rest. I constantly think and worry about everything. Trying to stay a step ahead of my coworkers and my enemies. Mentally exhausting.

Yeah, I walked by the medicine cabinet in the basement. I took two sedatives from the emergency staff medication supplies to calm my thoughts. It took the edge off. It made me feel normal—myself again. I was going and going and going on top of it again. It felt good. I was back.

But then, 24 hours later, the symptoms returned. I returned to the basement medicine cabinet, and this time, I took ten pills. No one would know. They were never counted in the daily tally of medication and were just considered extra. The only two people with the key were the head nurse and me. Those 10 pills got me back on my game. I was good for five days, and then I was a wreck. I started having chills. I was up all night, sweating, confused, unstable, and miserable. Unable to function.

I needed to go into the office on Saturday. Since I normally have weekends off, I would have to explain my presence to the head nurse, Tony. I needed to pull it together so I could get to the basement. All I needed was more pills. It was a gravity pull that I could not deny.

I walked into the building wearing black shades that camouflaged my bloodshot eyes and deep circles. I walked in calmly. I walked past several nurses, who said, "Hi." I smiled and waved.

Once I passed them, I rushed to my office and locked the door.

"Ok, you made it this far. Pull it together."

I got to the elevators unnoticed. The doors opened, and I could see the cabinet through the basement office window. I opened and closed the door behind me, taking one more look to make sure I was unobserved.

My body trembles. I take the key out and unlock the cabinet with a sweaty hand. How many pills should I take this time? I take the top off, hesitate, put the top back on, and caress the bottle between my breasts. A calmness comes over me. I glance around, open the bottle, and take three pills at once. I've gone from one pill to three pills. I know better than to increase your dosage. Once you do that, you're flirting with addiction. I'm feeling awfully good now. Better than normal. It's an immediate high.

With a smile, I run my back up and down the cabinet as if flirting with it. My mind already felt good. Now, I was out of body. I'm so happy because I know what to expect. In a little while, I'll be myself again, back on top of the world.

No one will find out. I already feel so much better. I have my stride back, my head up high, and my confidence is back. I can tackle anything that comes my way. Bring it!

With the remaining pills stashed away, I exited the hospital. As I headed to my car, I gripped my purse, holding it as if my life depended on it. Head Nurse Tony stopped me and said, "I checked in the basement office last week and noticed several pills were missing from the supply we keep in the cabinet."

"When I last checked, the meds were fine. You must have made a mistake in your count. Don't worry about it. I will double-check when I return on Monday."

"Sure, but I'm almost positive I counted correctly."

"No worries. I will recount on Monday. OK? Have a good weekend."

"You too, Tabby."

I just bit the bullet. What am I going to do now? How can I continue? As soon as I get home, I'll take some of my pills to help the three that I took earlier. Now, I'm taking two pills every two hours. I need them. I need them.

As I drive home, I notice in my review mirror a car following me. Is that one of my jealous coworkers trying to end my career? I pull up in the driveway, jump out of the car, and run into the house. Shut the door and lock it. They won't be able to get in. They won't be able to get me. I peek out of the curtain from the side. I thought I saw someone. Who? Who is that watching me from outside? That's someone from my job. It has to be. Who else could it be? My job is spying on me. I saw the bushes move. They are behind the bushes. I know someone got into my home and put cameras in the house. Where are those cameras? I'm going to tear this house up until I find them. Every drawer and cabinet. Behind plants, behind books, behind mirrors, behind couches, underneath the pillows, underneath beds, behind dressers. I tear the place up.

I don't find anything. OK, no cameras, microphones, or recording devices. I bet they won't get inside anymore. I place a chair behind the front door and the back door. I stay up all night and wait for them to break in. They are after me. They are trying to destroy me. They want to take my life away from me. How do I stop them? My mind is taking me all over the place.

"Mama? Mama, where are you? You always knew what to do."

I walked all night back and forth, with a bat in my hand, just in case. I was trying to see if any of the hospital nurses were near. I never caught anyone outside so far. I've been up all night on the lookout. It's already daylight. I see no one.

"Calm down Tabby girl."

It's already Monday morning. I'm a hot mess—sweaty, dirty, and musty as a muskrat. I need a shower. I have to pull myself together, clean myself up to enter the hospital, and face my enemies.

I take three pills to get through the morning. Place an ice bag over my puffy eyes. Then pull my braids back into a ponytail. Pour myself a cup of strong black coffee. That always does the trick. Here I go. Superwoman.

I get to my parking space and park. Then, as I get out of the car, a female security officer says, "Good morning. I've been ordered to escort you to the CEO's office."

"Why"

"Everything will be answered once we get there."

I almost wet my pants. All kinds of things are racing through my mind. The CEO knows. He doesn't know. He knows.

To save face and embarrassment, we use the back entrance, take the elevator, and finally arrive at the CEO's office.

"Hello, Jim, what's going on? You wanted to see me."

"Yes, I do. You have been the rising star for years and made the nursing department the best it has ever been. Our excellent reputation in the state is because of the protocols and procedures you put in place. You single-handedly built up the morale between nurses and doctors. You set and maintained the bar high. But it has come to my attention that medication is missing from the medical supply cabinet. Specifically, narcotics. All you need to say to me is that you did not take them. And the case will be closed. Take off your sunglasses. And tell me the truth."

I sit down, remove my sunglasses, pause momentarily, and look at the floor before raising my chin and speaking.

"We have never lied to each other; we've always been straightforward. Truthful. Over the years, I have been fortunate to call you a friend. Not just a person I work for."

I look once more at the floor. I sit up straight and slowly raise my head to look directly into his piercing blue eyes, my voice cracking.

"Yes, Jim, I have a problem."

He reached his hand out to mine as his tears fell. Seeing him cry made my tears fall—two people who genuinely respect and care for each other.

"I will not contact the police, but you must surrender your badge and keys, leave, and never set foot on hospital property again."

I complied, got up with my head held high, whispered, "Thank you," and exited his office.

He let me keep my dignity and self-respect. I walked down the back entrance and exited the hospital, never to return.

The achievements, recognition, social status, and wonderful life I had fought hard to make real were gone. In the blink of an eye. And there before me was Mama's face. Floating in front of me. She looked so real. Tears flowed as she clasped her hands at her breasts. I don't know if those tears I saw were embarrassment, shame, or pity. I will never know.

Then the tailspin begins. I continue to take the pills daily. Unopened bills. Foreclosed home. Personal items auctioned. My diamonds. Gone. My pearls. Gone. My designer shoes, gold bracelets, and 4-carat diamond ring that cost me $7,000 out the door. Gone. I purchased the ring during a time when I finally felt like I could treat myself, my reward. I was worthy of buying something of such caliber. That was for me. All gone. The love of my life, my BMW gone. Poof!

It all happened so fast. The sheriff came and escorted me out of what was no longer my home and padlocked the door. I did have a few possessions I was able to retrieve.

I sat on the steps of the home I no longer owned and sank deep into depression as my dream became my nightmare. This can't be happening. I worked for many years, being responsible, loyal, and dependable, doing everything right, focusing on my career, and foregoing a family and children because I wanted a successful career. I did it. I was successful. I met my goal!

And now, it's all gone. I have nothing to show for my previous life. I don't even have a piece of a leaf from my potassium plant. That was my baby, and it cost $2,500. Oh, how I loved her. She was placed near a bay window. She always had lots of sun in the morning and shade at sunset. My baby girl thrived. I called her Tutu. Gone.

I got up, started walking the streets, and found a low-budget motel, which helped me preserve the little money I had left in the bank.

I have $3,000 left to my name—pennies to me.

What am I going to do? How will I support myself? How will I put money on my sister's books? How would I explain my fall from grace? She looks up to me. All these thoughts are racing through my mind. The mind of a low budget pill junkie. Not in a specific order, just all over the place. I was supposed to be perfect and have it all together forever.

What is perfect? What does that look like?

Counting my pennies, I think this motel is not the best, but not the worst, at $99 a night. I gave the man $1,400 for two weeks. The room had a kitchenette, coffee, a microwave, and a little refrigerator. At least I can buy a few groceries and not have to eat out.

Thankfully, it has no bed bugs. I checked the mattress corners, an old trick Mama taught me. I have no roaches either. I'm not in the worst neighborhood, but I'm not in the best. At least no one is shooting dice or selling drugs in front of my door.

With all these pills in my system, I'm not supposed to feel, but I do. I can't stop crying. I'm still taking pills. I'm in trouble, I know. The pills have consumed me. They have taken me captive as their slave. You have no idea what I'm talking about if you haven't experienced your own fight with drugs.

There are days I don't sleep or eat. My body craves the pills. I've been united with them; as the Bible says, we are one flesh. I ought to know better, and I do, but I don't change. My life has been nothing but the study of medicine. The pros and cons. That's why it's truly a tragedy. I kept all my nurses on track, and now look at me. A drug addict and all alone. Who would imagine this as my fate? Even though I don't believe in it, some people say karma is what goes around comes back around with a vengeance. I don't know, but look at me. My specific look, all my swag is gone. No closet full of name brands with tags. No car. No fancy restaurants. No job perks. No place to lay my head down. No home. Now, I'm homeless.

Defeated.

That's what I am.

I have $1,400 left in my savings once I pay the next two weeks here. Then I will have nothing left.

The following two weeks came and went. I was out of funds. They had all dried up. The motel manager was adamant that I had to pack up and leave. I grabbed my little belongings and stepped out the door.

I looked around, and now I'm one of them. The very people I used to despise. I thought somehow they were in the way and stopping those like me from getting ahead. I do not want them near me, but now I am them, and they are me.

I'm shaking and sweating. I'm trying not to take the pills anymore. But the withdrawal is worse. It's like my insides are exploding. I want to vomit. I don't want to do it, but if I don't, then it will get worse.

I walk around all day. My feet started to swell. As I left, my Gucci tennis shoes cost $450. I sold a pair of diamond stud earrings for $400.00. That got me some blankets, a tent, a pillow, cheap tennis shoes, a scarf, socks, a heat pad, a white pocketknife, and food items. I knew I would camp out in the park with the rest of "those people."

I can't forget the essentials: small kitchen plastic bags and toilet paper. Yes, I have been reduced to using the bathroom in a plastic bag, and it's awful. But it's my new normal.

I have to be practical. I had a $100 bill left, and I was aware enough to know I had to get a game plan. I'm not completely gone. But it feels like it at times. I know I have to get off those pills, or I will eventually die in my tent or somebody's broken-down car. I couldn't let that happen, so I knew from my training that one week of cold Turkey would be the worst week of my life. But I had to. I wanted to save myself.

Thank goodness I was surrounded by wonderful, decent people I met in the park. Now, as I talked to many people and heard individual stories, I understand. It's horrible. It's unfair. There is no help for the poor and those victimized by the system, and they are unfairly judged by those who cease to really see them.

I ask Candy and Pop to watch over me. I didn't want to go to one of those detox center programs so instead I went "cold turkey."

I started that night shaking, with fever, chills, and vomiting all night.

Candy would get up, check on me, and throw away the vomit and the waste material bags for me. She kept me covered for warmth.

I remember one day, as I felt like dying, I begged Pop,"

"Please give me a pill."

"I can't do that. You can do this. You are better than this life. You are somebody. You are not us."

I remember those were the exact words Mama used to say.

I barely held on some nights. I would vomit so much that it made me weak; I couldn't lift my head to eat a piece of bread or even drink some water or take a sip of broth. But Candy spoon-fed me while lifting my head softly with a hand placed just so under my head as a tender mother would do for her young child. They watched over me like a hawk. No one got close to me or my tent.

I also lost the color of my skin. I was gray, even though I usually had a dark complexion. The grayness lasted a full two weeks. Then, I started turning the corner. My skin color came back. I stopped vomiting. I was able to hold down food. The shaking, fever, and sweating dissipated.

I started feeling like my old self. I don't believe I had seen the sun for an entire week. I was in my tent night and day. After seven days stuck inside, I finally exited my tent. The fresh air hit me in the face. For the first time, I had hope.

I started taking short walks with Candy and Pops, then longer and longer walks as part of the process. But we got through it together. They held my hand the whole way through.

Others in the camp would bring me food and water. It was our little community—nothing I had ever witnessed or experienced before. This is what family felt like. I had not felt like this since Mama died. Once again, I have a physically loving family. I belong to it.

As I continued to get better and stronger, my mind rebounded.

I promised Candy and Pop they would one day have a home with me and that I would take care of them for the rest of their lives. They said, "Oh, baby girl, even if that never happens, we love you always."

I also told the rest of the group that they would have their own one day, a home they could call their own.

"The streets will not be your 'forever home.' You are all somebody. I'm going to get you off of the streets. I mean that."

Now, I had to figure out how to get back on top. What do I want for myself? Think, woman, think. I figured this out this whole week. I was going to be the Chief Executive Officer of Landry Hospital, the same hospital that forced me to resign. I know, it's a tall order, but I can do it.

I told Candy and Pops about my new goal, and they supported me. I had no more money.

Most of the group had disability checks monthly. Some folks drank a little too much, but there were no drugs of any sort allowed in this community.

Candy and Pops got me a bucket of a car with smashed headlights.

The paint was peeling. The right-side mirror was gone, but the tags were current, and it was mine. It's not what I'm used to, but it was given to me out of love and necessity. That allowed me to drive to the library every day. Seven days a week. Week after week, I studied the ins and outs of the hospital's operation, from managing nurses, doctors' procedures, and outsourcing information. All staffing-related procedures, and how to run a hospital the size of Landry.

I studied with my little lamp inside the tent. One night, when I came back from sitting all day at the library, it was around midnight, and I could hear some movement outside my tent. I was quiet, and then finally, I turned the light off. I heard a sound like someone was in front of my tent. Then I heard my tent zipper slowly going up. I screamed. Then the karate chains came. They all came forward. They were not playing. The guy who tried to enter my tent and molest me left running. Nothing ever happened like that again. Everyone had each other's backs. I have never seen this before. I knew I had to get myself and them off the streets because the streets were unpredictable and unsafe.

Night and day, for a solid year, I studied and studied until one day I could finally take the test at Tracy Myers hospital. You could take the test to become a CEO if you felt you could pass the test without going to a two-year program.

The test was held on Friday, June 16th, at 9:30 AM. It would last until 3:30 PM and be a six-hour session with two 10-minute breaks and one 30-minute meal break. I felt ready. I prayed. Then I remembered one of Momma's sayings: "You can be anything you want to be. Only you can stop you."

You are right, Mama.

On the day of the exam, I sat and looked around. Six Caucasian men, three Caucasian women, and one black woman, me, are taking the exam. The proctor explained the rules. The timer was set for two hours, then 11:30, a 10-minute break, and I stretched in the hallway. When the 10 minutes were over, we all returned to our seats.

The timer went off again after two hours. It was time for our 30-minute meal break. Pops and Candy brought me a sandwich, chips, a drink, and my favorite strawberries in a brown paper bag. I thought, how sweet.

During the break, my mind kept wandering. I did OK on the last part of the test period. I passed. I knew I gave it my all. The 30-minute break is over, and the final hour and a half is all that's left.

The timer starts, and the test begins.

I'm going back and forth with answers, erasing several. I knew/know *(?)* I was incorrect. I made the proper corrections. The last question was personal.

"Why do you want to be CEO of any company?"

I thought hard and long, and I answered it like this.

I want to be CEO because I want to make a difference to all the patients and family members who come through the hospital doors for help. I want them to know we care and that all lives matter. They will always be treated with respect and compassion and left with their dignity. I want the staff to feel valued, seen, and heard.

Then the timer went off, and the pencils went down. The proctor spoke.
"Hand in your papers. The test scores will be posted on the bulletin board in two hours, at 5:30 PM."

I kept doubting myself. Did I do enough? Did I read through every question before I answered? My mind was racing. I couldn't eat—I just had a bottle of water—and my nerves were shot. I kept looking at my watch every 15 minutes. Those two hours became the longest of my life.

It's 5:30 PM.

I walked slowly into the building and headed to the basement. I looked on the board for my name, Tabby Thomas, and there it was. My finger dragged very slowly to the end of the line where my grade was posted. Just before I reached the end, I closed my eyes and then opened them.

97.8

I could not believe it. I dropped to my knees in front of everyone, looked up, and thanked Mama. I had the highest grade of all the participants, male or female!

I drove back home, ignoring all speed limits. I just wanted to get back to my family, and they were there.

It's cupcakes and BBQ for my celebration. For one day, we were not homeless. They knew. They believed in me. We did a group hug. We danced, we ate, and we laughed together.

The interview for the CEO position in the area was on Monday. I was ashamed and a little sad. Pop said, "What's wrong, baby girl?"

"I have no clothes appropriate for the interview."

"Who says you don't?"

He went and got a huge square box and gave it to me.

"This is for you from us."

I opened it. I found a black blazer with a matching skirt, a beige long-sleeve blouse with a bow tie on the side, black stockings, black and white pointed-toe sling-back pumps, and a black, white, and red purse. I just cried. I kept my head down. Pops said, "Don't you ever hold your head down again."

I kissed every one of them—my family. I love them all.

Monday came so fast. Candy asked, "Do you want to catch a cab for your interview?"

"No, I don't. I'm going to drive the car that was given to me with love. I'm not ashamed."

She kissed my forehead. I got in the car and waved.

I arrived 20 minutes early for my interview. They gave me a form that required my current address and contact information. Thank goodness I had gotten a P.O. Box at Candy's suggestion. I filled out the forms and handed them back. I sat with my heart in my stomach.

"Tabby Thomas? Mr. Reynolds will see you now."

I walked in and gave him my test scores. He looked directly at me without blinking and asked me very specific questions. Staffing and interpersonal relationships for discipline issues and racial conflicts are heavy topics, and I had to think quickly on my feet.

I was in there for 45 minutes. He shook my hand.

"I will contact you with our decision and the hospital where you will be stationed if you are hired."

"Thank you for your time and for allowing me to be part of this hiring process."

As I got into the elevator, Mr. Reynolds ran out of the office and said, "Wait, Miss Thomas. You have the job. You are the new CEO of Landry Hospital on West 3rd. Do you know anything about that hospital?"

"I'm familiar with that hospital."

"Come back to my office so we can talk about the specifics of the job."

I went back to his office, and I have to admit, it was extremely hard not to jump up and scream with joy! Instead, I sat quietly and professionally as he went into the specifics.

"Due to an unexpected retirement, we must fill this position immediately. Which means there is a hiring bonus of $50,000. The position comes with a three-bedroom, three-bath home located not too far from the hospital. Here are the keys. The address is 205 N Sierra Rd. Your starting salary is $275,000 a year. Welcome aboard, Miss Thomas."

"Thank you so much. Mr. Reynolds, you won't regret your decision."

"I know. Can you start Friday?"

" Yes, I can."

 Happy tears stream down my face as I exit his office. My nose is running. I can't believe it. I go home. I ran and screamed, "I got the job. I did it. We did it."

We did our famous group hug. There was not a dry eye to be found.

"Pops and Candy, start packing and get ready to move. Throw those tents away. Bring only the special things and group, you guys start packing too."

I have four days to locate an eight-person apartment with four bedrooms and three baths. The money was already transferred to my previous bank account for $50,000. I called the realtor I knew back in the day. Sherry got it right on it. I told her what I was looking for. I wanted it to be close to my current home. Two days later, she showed me a four-bedroom three-bath duplex first-floor apartment for $2800 a month, one street over from my new home. I wrote her a check for $33,600, covering their rent for one year.

First, I helped Pop and Candy. On Wednesday, with their little belongings in my car, I told them to close their eyes. I got them out of the car and told them to keep their eyes closed. I opened the door and told them to open their eyes. Candy screamed, and Pop fell to the ground; he had never been inside something so beautiful. I told him to look around.

I went upstairs to the master suite. There was a beautiful soaker tub, a huge shower, a massage unit, a double vanity, a walk-in closet in the bathroom, a bedroom makeup room, and a large balcony with a beautiful view. I went downstairs, and Candy said, "This is a beautiful home for you."

"What do you mean? This is your home too. Grab the huge bedroom with the bathroom on the left; it's yours. You guys are officially my adoptive parents."

We all cry.

"Yes, this is ours. I will care for you for the rest of your lives, Mom and Dad. Mom cook whatever you want in your kitchen. Dad, shower and turn on sports; I'll be back. Oh, and here's your set of keys. As I left, I turned, and they said, "Goodbye, daughter."

"Don't make me cry some more. See you guys soon."

I went back to the camp to get the rest of my family.

"OK, let's go."

"Where are we going, girl?"

"Don't bring those tents. Throw them into the garbage bin. Joe, stop being stubborn. Tents are not needed anymore. Cat, Karen, Slick Joe, Roy, Tammy, and Chris, let's go, guys. We have to bundle together inside the car."

"Where are you taking us, girl?"

"Just wait, Cat. You will see there's no better tent park in this town."

Roy said, "I know something better."

I pulled up to 2229 Cordoba Way, Unit B. Everyone got out of the car and stared at the building in front of them.

"Ok, everyone, form a straight line. Good. Now, grab the hand of the person in front of you. Now close your eyes. No peeking. I mean it."

I grab the hand of the person at the front of the line and lead them into the building.

"Now open."

"Oh, what a beautiful place."

"I love your place. Maybe we can visit one day."

"No, you can't…because this place is yours! Two of you can share a room."

"This is ours?"

"Yes. No more tents. No more sleeping in the cold rain. You guys can be here forever. Now you have to work as a team, just as you did before, to keep your apartment clean. I will be inviting myself, Candy, and Pops for dinner. We are just on the next block over."

Everyone cried.

"Oh, I forgot. Here are eight sets of keys. This is yours for as long as you want."

We did a group hug. I kiss everybody on the forehead.

"OK, boy, you are a little funky. Take a long bath. And Joe, please do the same. You all have new clothes in the closet. The refrigerator is stocked with food. Also, next week, you guys have a special surprise in store."

"We could never pay you back."

"You already have by loving me."

As I turned to leave, they said, "We love you!"

"I love you, too! You guys get used to your new living quarters."

I closed the door behind me. It was a job well done. The people who meant the most to me are safe in Bradford.

I go home and get ready for Friday. I open the door and call for Mom and Pops. There is no answer. I go into the room, and they are sleeping on the floor with blankets and a pillow. I leave them. It will take them time to get used to their new life. The streets have a way of sticking to you. You don't believe they do, but they really do.

I go upstairs to my room and fall onto my bed. I look up at the ceiling and say, "This is mine. I'm back."

The introduction is tomorrow. I'm going to wear the same outfit that got me the job. My first meeting is a full circle. The same situation as my first hospital meeting is repeated. The outgoing CEO and everyone have no idea it's me. My meeting is at 9:00 AM sharp. I park in the back. I go into the building where I was last escorted out, now entering the back entrance, up the elevator, into conference room B. I take a deep breath and say a quick prayer. I slowly turned the knob and opened the door. I wait to walk in. I exhale. As I walked in, all mouths fell to the ground, and pencils and pens fell to the table. Shock has overtaken them.

"Hello, my name is Tabby Thomas. I'm the new CEO. Let's get started. The applause starts small as the surprise wears off and builds into everyone smiling, clapping enthusiastically, and cheering!.

Jim Cook rushes over, and we embrace each other. He whispers, "I knew you would be back."

To the group, he says, "Let's welcome your new CEO."

A spontaneous standing ovation surrounds me with warmth.

"Thank you, it's good to be back."

I take my seat. This time, my feet are planted, rooted in the ground solidly. I looked quickly above and said, "This is for you, Mama. I'm back. I am somebody."

The moral of the story is that everyone can fall from grace, but it takes humility and courage to find your way back. You remember the lessons learned on the way back up. Somebody is always somebody, whether rich or poor. All lives matter.

EMAIL

2424Belinda@gmail.com

PUBLISHING COMPANY

www.AngelGirlPublications.com

Made in the USA
Las Vegas, NV
27 April 2025

21432041R00026